MRS. TIGGY-WINKLE

Based on the original story by
Beatrix Potter
with all new illustrations

Cover illustration by
Anita Nelson
Book illustrations by
Sam Thiewes

Publications International, Ltd.

Once there was a little girl named Lucie who lived on a farm. She was a good little girl, but she was always losing her pocket handkerchiefs!

One day little Lucie came into the farmyard crying that she had lost three handkerchiefs and a pinafore! She asked Tabby Kitten and Sally Henny-Penny if they had found her handkerchiefs, but they hadn't.

Lucie looked up at the hillside. She thought she saw some white things spread upon the grass.

Lucie scrambled up the hill along a steep pathway—up and up. Soon she came to a bubbling spring. Where the sand upon the path was wet, there were footprints of a very small person.

The path ended under a big rock. There were clotheslines of braided grasses and a heap of tiny clothespins on the ground. But there were no handkerchiefs!

There was something else, though—a door! It led straight into the hill, and beyond it someone was singing.

Lucie's knock interrupted the song. A frightened little voice called out, "Who's there?" Lucie opened the door to a nice, clean, very small kitchen.

There, with an iron in her hand, stood a short, plump person wearing a large apron over her striped petticoat. Her little black nose went sniffle, and her eyes went twinkle. And under her cap—where Lucie had yellow curls—the little person had PRICKLES!

Lucie asked, "Who are you? Have you seen my pocket handkerchiefs?"

The little person curtsied. "Yes, miss. My name is Mrs. Tiggy-Winkle." She ironed a little red vest. "That's belonging to Cock Robin," she said.

"There's one of my handkerchiefs!" cried Lucie. "And there's my pinafore!"

Mrs. Tiggy-Winkle ironed the pinafore and shook out the ruffles.

"Oh, that is lovely!" said Lucie.

Lucie asked about some yellow
gloves. "Oh, no!" said the little
person, "that's a pair of stockings
belonging to Sally Henny-Penny. And
the red handkerchief, if you please,
miss, is old Mrs. Rabbit's. It did
smell so of onions. And that's a pair
of mittens belonging to Tabby Kitten.
I only have to iron them, she washes
them herself."

"Here are my handkerchiefs!" said
Lucie. At last the basket was empty.

After they had sorted the wash, Mrs. Tiggy-Winkle made tea. She and Lucie sat on a bench in front of the fire and looked at one another.

Mrs. Tiggy-Winkle's hands were very, very brown, and very, very wrinkly from the soapsuds. And all through her gown and cap there were hairpins sticking wrong end out. When they had finished tea, they tied up the clothes in bundles. Lucie's handkerchiefs were folded up inside her clean pinafore.

Then away down the hill trotted Lucie and Mrs. Tiggy-Winkle with the bundles of clothes. All the way down the path little animals came out of the woods to meet them. The very first they met were Peter Rabbit and Benjamin Bunny!

Mrs. Tiggy-Winkle and Lucie gave them all their nice clean clothes. The little animals and birds were very grateful to dear Mrs. Tiggy-Winkle.

At the bottom of the hill they came to the garden steps. There was nothing left to carry except Lucie's one little bundle.

Lucie scrambled up the steps with the bundle in her arms. Then she turned to say "Good night" and to thank the washerwoman.

But how very odd! Mrs. Tiggy-Winkle had not waited for thanks.

She was running, running up the hill—and where was her white ruffled cap? And her petticoat and gown? How small and brown she seemed— and covered with PRICKLES! Why, Mrs. Tiggy-Winkle was nothing but a HEDGEHOG!

Now some people say that little Lucie had been dreaming. But what about her clean handkerchiefs and pinafore? And besides—I have seen that door in the hill. And I am a good friend of dear Mrs. Tiggy-Winkle!